God in the Midst of Finding Grace

Raul Romero

Copyright © 2024 Raul Romero

God's Grace Romero Books —Bartlett, TN
ISBN: 979-8-218-47858-2
eBook ISBN: 979-8-3303-5132-9
Library of Congress Control Number: 2024917106
Title: *God in the Midst of Finding Grace*
Author: Raul Romero
Digital distribution | 2024
Paperback | 2024

Other books by Raul Romero

Looking for a Humble Servant

I am the door. If anyone enters by me, he will be saved.

Dedication

To my loving wife Tammy who has been an inspiration in my life. Her supportive prayers and encouragement has kept me on the path towards the cross. Thank you, Honey.

To my community group, Rick, Cindy, Joe, Marlane, Larry, Donna, Mark, Barbara, Dale, Pamela, Judy, Steve, Brenda, Pat, Carol, Doug, Frank, and Frances. When we meet every month, you are my prayer warriors. You pray for us continually. Thank you.

I want to thank Dr. Tim Foster, Pastor of Highland Heights Presbyterian Church, Memphis, Tennessee, and Commander in the United States Navy Reserve, for taking the time to explain to me what is involved in training a military Chaplain.

Table of Contents

Author's Note

While writing this book, I think about my relationship with God and how I need to grow closer to Him. I pray daily for wisdom, humbleness, mercy, encouragement, and grace. I thank you for taking the time to read and hope that you enjoy this fiction story. Maybe it will encourage you to write a story - you never know. What is your story? In this book, I write about a Pastor and his walk with God. Years of tragedy, loss, and anger changed his heart to bitterness. In the end, God had been working all the time in his life and ended his anger by finding Grace.

Chapter 1
Walking and Talking with God

Deuteronomy 5:33 (NIV)
"Walk in all the ways that the Lord your God has commanded you, so that you may live and prosper and prolong your day in the land that you will possess."

James Robinson had just graduated from high school in the town of Missoula. James was a smart student and could attend any college he wanted, due to his outstanding scores and graduating with top honors. He had aced the ACT and had taken various tests for possible entry into the military.

Each military branch was looking for this young man, hoping to enroll him in top-notch programs. He was the elite package. He was also one of the best quarterbacks in football, and several colleges had offered him a full scholarship. James was an athletic young man. His future looked bright. His mom and dad were very proud of him. His father, Pastor Rick Robinson, was the pastor of a church that had about three hundred members. His mother, April Robinson, was active in the community and ran several programs in the church. His older brother Eddie had graduated from Montana Seminary and was pastoring a church in San Francisco. His sister Susie had moved to New York and had married a pastor. She graduated from college with an engineering degree.

James was the youngest of the children and had been raised in church and had also decided his life calling was to become a pastor, just like his dad. Pastor Rick was excited that his youngest son had also chosen to serve God. When he eventually asked James why, he chose to become a pastor, James told his Dad that God had walked and talked to him so that he could serve Him. Rick of course, hugged his son, and both had tears of joy. In that very moment they felt like Jesus had wrapped His arms around them. When they were done, Dad said, "Let's have dinner and see what mom has cooked."

Mom had cooked James' favorite meal - chicken casserole, biscuits, corn on the cob, and four-layer-delight pie. The family came together that evening like a painting that Thomas Kinkaid would probably have been proud to paint, beautiful and serene. In America today, that picture of families gathering at the table is gone and on these occasions, there was far too much technology, with children even looking at their phones or video playing games at the dinner table. There often, is little reverence to God or saying Grace.

When they had finished dinner, Dad went into his study to read and meditate on God's word and James went to help his mom clean up in the kitchen, and thank her for the fabulous dinner.

Mom just smiled...tears rolling down her cheeks. Sharing this time together with her son was coming to an end. After cleaning up, James hugged his mom and left the room to see his dad. Dad had just finished reading Deuteronomy 5:13 and wanted to share this verse with his son.

"Remember this verse, and hold it close to your heart. God will show you the way and prepare the fields before you."

Rick had also asked James what he was going to do during his last summer in his hometown, and James told him that he would be working at the local hardware store with his girlfriend, Elizabeth.

Both had been working at the store for a very long time and this was the place where they had first started to notice each other. Both were saving their money to start a future, together. They planned to set the funds aside for a down payment on a new home, wherever God lead them to settle down. Their friendship had grown, and they became high school sweethearts. They both wanted to abstain from any sexual contact until they were married and had made a vow of chastity to each other and to God.

It was very hard for James, because as a good-looking young man many of the ladies in the high school wanted to date him. He was popular, and the other teammates would always pressure him to go to parties. Often, at these events they would get drunk, and some boys would take advantage of the girls. James would always step in to help and volunteer to remove the young ladies from those situations by driving them home. He finally decided not to attend any more parties. Every time there was a temptation, he would take time to pray and seek God's guidance, praying to get him out of bad situations. He would remember 1 Corinthians 10:13, "But when you are tempted, He will also provide a way out so that you can stand up under it."

James and Elizabeth worked almost every day at the hardware store, and they were well-liked by their co-workers and the owner. They would work the second shift from four to ten o'clock on weekdays and would work an occasional Saturday, the same hours that they worked during the week.

On Saturday, James always took Elizabeth home in his 1968 red Mustang convertible, riding down Main Street, and then driving down one of those long and beautiful scenic country roads. They would turn on the radio to listen to Christian music and would sing together. Both were blessed with wonderful voices.

As they were heading a drunk driver crashed into them in a head-on collision. James was in a coma for several weeks and had both legs broken, a broken left arm, and several bruises on his face. Unfortunately, this brought his athletic career to an end. When he finally woke up and could speak and gather his thoughts, his family was beside him and his siblings had flown in, due to the accident. He immediately asked for Elizabeth, but his mom had said to get some rest and that he would be updated on her status. Nobody could bring themselves to let him know that Elizabeth had died on the scene from the impact. Finally, on the third day, her dad Erik, had come in to let James know that Elizabeth did not make it. He screamed and sobbed uncontrollably, at hearing the news and blamed himself for letting it happen.

Erik held James close, and told him that it was not his fault. He explained what happened since James could not remember anything about the accident. It was a long and arduous task to recover from, and he was eventually transitioned to a rehabilitation facility. Unfortunately, James had to skip his first year of college.

At the rehabilitation center, endured arduous rounds of physical therapy every day, and would yell from the pain as he tried to take small steps as he learned to walk again. He otherwise used a wheelchair to get around for the next few months. While in recovery, he spent more time reading and memorizing Bible verses. He asked God to fill him with His love and guide him through the recovery process. He witnessed to other patients and read to the elderly passages from the Bible. All the staff and patients started to fall in love with James. One Sunday the chaplain from the facility got so sick that he could not preach the Sunday service, so he asked the staff to ask James if he could preach for him. When Nancy the head nurse knocked on James' door, she explained the situation and he gladly accepted even though he was not a pastor yet. He planned to use the opportunity to spread the love of Jesus Christ.

He decided to speak on *Refreshing My Walk with Jesus* based on 1 John 5-10. The outline of his talk was: Walk in the light, Walk with one another, and Walk in forgiveness. After he had finished his sermon, he was so nervous, but all the patients and staff came up to him and told him what a wonderful job he had done. That made him feel so good. After being at the physical therapy facility for about two months, it was time to go home. It was a sad day for the patients who were there, because they were going to miss his readings and the times he told them about God's love. His parents brought him home that day. His dad had turned his study room into a temporary bedroom for James, so that he would not have to climb the stairs. One day, while he was watching television, there was a knock at the front door. His mom told the person at the door that he should not be there. James came around the corner to see who it was. It was the man who had crashed his car into James' car. He was escorted by two guards. He was on his way to prison and wanted to ask James for his forgiveness. James told the man he could come in.

The man sobbed, and he told James that he had come to know Jesus and wanted to make peace with him and with Elizabeth's family. James prayed with the man and they both started crying. They embraced, and the man left to serve his sentence.

Chapter 2
New Beginnings

Isaiah 43-18-19 (NIV)
"Forget the former things; do not dwell on the past. See, I am doing a new thing. Now it springs up; do you not perceive it? I am making a way in the desert and streams in the wasteland."

Finally, the day had arrived, and he said goodbye to his mom and dad. He had saved some money from all the work he had done, and he purchased a Rubicon, a big boys' Jeep, so that he could drive in any type of weather while in college. He made one last stop at the town cemetery to look at Elizabeth's grave to say goodbye. On the beautiful marble headstone there was a saying, "Blessed are the merciful, for they shall obtain mercy" (Matthew 5:7).

As he walked, he had envisioned Elizabeth walking beside him, so they could attend seminary together. He paused and said with a whisper, "I miss you and one day I will see you again. You will always be in my heart. Goodbye, Elizabeth."

It was the fall semester in late August as he drove into the picturesque college campus. He had a piece of paperwork and directions that led him to his new quarters for the next four years. As he checked into the office, he got his room keys and a packet that had the college map to get him acquainted with the college campus, buildings and most importantly the school cafeteria.

As he entered carrying a multitude of boxes and bumping into other first-year students, it was quite an obstacle to get to his room on the second floor. His room had a window overlooking a park with a big water fountain and, in the center, a cross with big, bold letters of a Bible verse, Mark 16:15: "Go into all the world and preach the good news to all creation."

James was very anxious to meet his roommate, but it was getting late, so he went to get something to eat at the local pizza place and as soon as he got there, he made some new friends. The owners Frank and Frances liked James, and they asked him if he wanted a job. He knew that he had to work to have some spending money and to put gas in his car. James took an application and told them that he would return it as soon as he got done with orientation and settling into his room. James was so thoughtful that he took five slices of pepperoni pizza and a large soda as a way to break the ice with his roommate.

As soon as he got to his room, a small young man of Spanish heritage greeted him with a hug and introduced himself with broken English as Alejandro Manuel Acosta Bonilla de Salazar. James smiled and thought to himself, what am I going to call him? James asked him if he was hungry, and he said yes. The young man had not eaten all day, and he scarfed down those five pieces of pizza in minutes. After he finished, he let out a big belch. James thought to himself, how does anything so loud come out of that little body? They both laughed and then got ready for bed. They had decided to finish arranging their room the next day after church. James had asked Alejandro if he wanted to go to church the next day, and he said, "Si (Yes)."

Alejandro was extremely nervous about attending an English-speaking church. He had a strong accent, and he was scared that people would make fun of the way he pronounced words. James realized that Alejandro was nervous due to his sweaty hands and non-stop talking. James told him it was going to be all right. "I will be with you," he said.

So, James asked Alejandro to pull out his Bible so they could read a passage and then pray for the day to come. He opened the Bible to Joshua 1:6, and Alejandro opened his English/Spanish version. "Be strong and courageous."

Alejandro said, "Oh, I like this passage very much, Fuerte y Valiente (strong/courageous)."

He said that this passage was read to him by his Lita - short for Abuelita. His Lita was not educated but she remembered stories told from the Bible that she had learned when she was young. Whenever Alejandro was afraid of something, she would remind him of this passage. Alejandro went back in time talking about his Lita. While making tortillas in an old clay oven, she would just start humming some songs that she had heard from the missionaries that had brought her to the Lord. She sold tortillas so that Alejandro could attend college in America and become a pastor for the village. All the village had pitched in to send Alejandro to get educated. Missionary groups would stop by the village and would teach English to Alejandro. He got so interested in the language that he would walk for miles to attend a local sponsored missionary school to get his education. He was extremely smart, and the missionary group wanted to help him get to college. Alejandro said that when God has a plan, He makes it happen and that was why he was here. James quickly prayed and said that they needed to get going to church and that they would have plenty of time to talk about his village and family later. Alejandro stared at James's eyes, which told him of his own transportation called terco (stubborn.) James was puzzled and he asked what kind of car it was.

"Oh," Alejandro said, "my four-legged burro."

They both laughed. There were several churches of various denominations in the town, and he had heard of a church called Life that was geared toward college students. It was a big church with about one thousand members and had several student ministries. Alejandro had never seen anything so big, and he kept bumping into James, because he was so distracted by the building. He told James that he could fit his whole village into this church. They both laughed. Then they were greeted and found their seats. The worship band began to play and sing a few songs to get the crowd on fire and set the tone for the Holy Spirit to fall upon the congregation. Alejandro did not know what to say when he heard the sound coming from the stage, and James saw his jaw hit the ground and snickered. The congregation started lifting their arms up to heaven in worship. James and his new Spanish friend were just at peace and giving God all the glory. After the music session had ended, a young youth pastor welcomed the congregation and the first-time visitors while information about the different programs offered by the church was being passed out. He also announced that the church was having lunch for all first-time visitors. James and Alejandro said Amen out loud, and the congregation laughed. The main pastor came up and prayed for the congregation and asked the congregation to open their Bibles to John 13: 12-17. The title of his sermon was "Washing the Feet of Sinners." He talked about his early ministry in which he found it easy to talk to people who attended church, but not the unsaved. He said God had humbled him and showed him this verse on which he was talking about today. After the passing of the buckets for tithing, the pastor was about to close when he asked the congregation if there was anyone in need of prayer, salvation, or recommitment.

He asked the congregation to bow their heads and asked those who needed salvation to lift their hand up and put it down. Several people in the congregation lifted their hand and then the pastor prayed the prayer of salvation for them. **"Lord Jesus, I confess that I am a sinner and in need of salvation. I ask for forgiveness of my sins. Cleanse me and make me whole again. You died on the cross for me as the substitute of my sins and on the third day you rose and now are seated at the right hand of God. Thank you for dying for me. Give me the strength to serve and walk with you for the rest of my life. In Jesus' name. Amen."**

Many young people came to the cross that day and it was a day that gave James and Alejandro strength to keep going and serve God, to be salt and light in the world. As they were heading towards the fellowship area of the church, James accidentally tripped over the foot of a young lady and fell. He quickly managed to get up and was so embarrassed, but quickly gained composure and was staring at a beautiful young lady who was apologizing and making sure that he was okay. James put on his macho mask and said that he was okay.

She introduced herself as Mandy and said she was from Colorado. It was her first year of college and she wanted to be a teacher and serve God in poor countries of the world. She wanted to teach impoverished children to read and write. That was Mandy's dream. James did not know what to say. He was staring at her beautiful blue eyes and golden hair. Her face was like that of a princess out of a movie. He was so intensely wrapped up in her beauty that he could not hear her voice, so she took hold of his arm and asked if he was okay. Alejandro quicky intervened, because he could see his friend's googly eyes looking at Mandy and said, "Despierta (Wake up)."

Mandy then continued walking down the hall, and James gave Alejandro the look of, "Why did you interrupt me?"

Alejandro laughed and said, "Come on, dreamer."

So, they both got their food, and James tried to find Mandy but couldn't. She had just gotten an apple and left for the day to get back to her dorm to study.

James could not finish his meal, because he was just thinking about Mandy, so Alejandro asked if he could eat his food also.

James said, "For a little man, you can put it away."

Alejandro laughed and said that this was so different from eating rice and beans.

Monday came, and it was the first day of classes. Alejandro had signed up for the same classes as James did so that James could help him with the work. Alejandro was not very fluent in reading and writing English, so he needed the help from James. So, James agreed to help Alejandro get through college and become a pastor so he could go back home to Guatemala and preach God's Word. James and Alejandro joined other students in groups so that they could make it together. Fortunately for James, Mandy had also joined the group and they started to develop a relationship. They shared a lot of classes together, and also studied together. James and Mandy took Spanish classes in case they ended up in a Spanish-speaking mission and to be able to speak with Alejandro and help him get through the years of college ahead of him. The second and third year went by kind of fast. All three of them made wonderful memories, and finally their senior year was approaching.

All three of them worked at a local hardware store in town to have spending money. Alejandro helped the Hispanic population and the store saw increased sales due to his presence as a sales associate. James and Mandy had fallen in love. James had met her family and they loved him. James had talked to Alejandro about how he felt about Mandy and had asked him to become his best man at the future wedding. So, James had been planning to take her to a picnic area overlooking the town and pop the question as the sun went down. He had prepared some sandwiches and all the picnic fixings and after he turned on the radio, they listened to a few Christian songs. They embraced, because they were in love. After relaxing for a few minutes, James got on his knees and asked her to marry him. Mandy was in tears, happy tears of course, and she said yes. They planned for the wedding to be in his hometown and wanted to have the reception in the backyard of his parents' home. They wanted to get married before they graduated so that they could be together in whatever God had in store for them.

The wedding took place during the Christmas holidays, and they were going to graduate in May of the following year. As it is with all colleges around the country, the armed forces came in and tried to recruit graduating pastors to be military chaplains. James was a candidate they were seeking, due to his scholastic achievements and because he had acquired his masters in pastoral counseling, discipleship and church ministry. James asked Mandy what she thought about him joining the Army. After each of them prayed and fasted on their own, they got together on a Saturday evening and lifted their prayer towards heaven. They felt the presence of the Holy Spirit and felt it was a sure sign that God was going to use them for His purposes in the armed services.

Chapter 3
Serving His Country

Deuteronomy 31:6 (NIV)
"Be strong and courageous. Do not fear or be in dread of them, for it is the LORD your God who goes with you. He will not leave you or forsake you."

On a beautiful Friday morning, James said goodbye to his wife Mandy and his mom and dad. He was off to Ft Jackson in Columbia, South Carolina for a 12-week Basic Officer Leadership Course and Chaplain School. There he would learn the noncombatant skills, Army etiquette and chaplain duties. James would also learn to minister to military personnel and their families and to work with local civilians within an area that is involved with military operations. He already possessed self-discipline and was in good physical condition. He, Mandy, and Alejandro always ran about five miles a day while in college. He loved to run, because it was a way to clear his mind and get ready for exams that would confront him that day. Alejandro played soccer so he needed to be conditioned to run all over the field and play once again in his village. James' first day involved checking into Personnel to begin receiving his military pay, to get his military identification card, to add Mandy as a dependent, and get his military record started. He was assigned to a barracks with other fellow future chaplains.

The process of checking in took about 3 days. He had to see medical and get all his immunizations up to date. He did not like that, because he was a little squeamish at the sight of a needle. He then got sent to dental for an examination. The dentist made an appointment for him to have all his wisdom teeth taken out. He also did not like that, but he agreed to it. After recuperating from the extractions and all the immunizations that he had received, he was ready to begin his training. James was a candidate to become an Army Chaplain and to do that, he had to attend a course which lasted 12 weeks. During this training he would learn to develop essential staff officer skills, basic chaplain ministry and pastoral skills to function as a chaplain at battalion level. The Army would train him and the other chaplains in his class to develop leadership and professionalism be used in the field.

Each new day of training began early in the morning with a long run with Staff Sergeant Miller and Sergeant First Class Rowdy. They both would come into the barracks banging a trash can lid along the long hallway and screaming at the top of their lungs. James and all the new recruits would scramble to come to attention and be ready for orders. They had three minutes to get into their physical training gear and then into formation. On the first day they started their two-mile run. As they were coming to the first mile mark, James began to see three of his friends slowing down, because they were not able to keep up with the rest of the company. They were not in shape yet and had some pounds to lose. Staff Sergeant Miller was trying to motivate them, but one of them named Arnie began to complain about pain in his legs. There was an Army medic truck following the group in order to pick up any injured recruit. Just as Arnie was about to give up, James came up beside him and had him lean against him while running. They both completed the run, and it was time for breakfast. What they did not know was that they would have to eat breakfast as they went through the line and what they didn't eat while they were going through the line, they had to dump in the garbage cans at the end of the line. The Staff Sergeant told the soldiers, "Welcome to McDonald's in the Army."

As soon as breakfast was over, they would go to attend classes all day. Before lights out was called, they were encouraged to write a letter home. James would write to Mandy about his day and tell her that he missed her and loved her so much. Mandy was always happy to receive a letter from James and she would read it to his parents. James' Mom would always have tears in her eyes, because her baby boy was in the Army. While James was away at officer training, Mandy would write about how she was helping James's mom and dad with church functions. She would type the weekly bulletin for the congregation and assist with meeting community needs with the homeless, those addicted to drugs and provide counseling to young females, who were involved in prostitution. She was also teaching part time at a foster center. She taught first and second graders, and all the children loved her. Her degree was in youth and children's ministry.

Phase One had begun with twelve officer candidates from different denominations and during this phase the focus was on developing essential staff officer skills to function in the Army. Phase Two provided essentials for the chaplain ministry and helped the candidates develop skills for pastoral function at the battalion level. Phase Three emphasized leadership and professionalism for officers in the field. Graduation came and orders were given to each officer.

Mandy and the commanding officer of the base had the privilege of pinning on James the rank of Captain (O3) due to his education and ministry experience he had prior to joining the Army.

The graduates were now able to go home and spend time with their families for two weeks before reporting to their first official duty stations. James was ordered to report to Fort Hood to be ready for deployment to Afghanistan to support Operation Enduring Freedom. The orders were for a battalion chaplain who was to report to the base once his leave was over.

His battalion had already been deployed to Kabul and he had to be deployed right away for a period of nine months. Mandy was heart-broken, because she could only spend a little time with her new officer. His parents and his wife gathered around him to pray for a hedge of protection over him. There were a lot of tears shed the night before he left, but they all knew his country needed him. He had no time to set up housing for Mandy and him at Fort Hood, so he asked his parents if she could stay a little longer with them. Of course, they said yes. So, he took a flight from Fort Hood to Kabul, Afghanistan.

It was a long flight of about 16 hours, so he found a cozy place to lay his head and prayed for the crew members, pilots, and support personnel. He wrote a letter to Mandy asking for forgiveness for it being such a short letter, but he promised to return home.

When they had landed in Kabul, he found out there was a 9-hour time difference. So, he asked his staff sergeant what a good time would be was to call the United States. He told him 0700 am Afghanistan time.

The next morning, he called Mandy to let her know that he had made it safe and sound. He could only stay on the phone for a while. He had to report to his superiors and get debriefed on the task at hand. The chapel was a makeshift tent with a few benches and an altar made from old wooden crates. In the middle was a cross made by the local children, and that put a smile on his face. He had a small office which he would use to counsel anyone who needed it. He had been a busy man since he had arrived and was trying to play catch up. As a chaplain, his job consisted of getting to know the troops and traveling to areas with Soldiers who had been in combat and needed spiritual support. One day the commanding officer had requested his presence to go to Khost area to hold services at Camp Chapman. He was to remain there for about two weeks. While he was there talking and encouraging military personnel, he came across a young corporal who was curled up in a corner getting some rest before he was going on his patrol around the town. What caught James' attention was that he was reading a small military Bible.

Chaplain Robinson introduced himself, asked the corporal what he was reading and sat down beside him. He was reading Isaiah 6:8: "Then I heard the voice of the Lord saying, 'Whom shall I send? And who will go for us?' And I said, 'Here am I. Send me.'" The Chaplain started a conversation by saying he noticed his last name was King.

"What is your first name?" he asked.

The corporal answered, "Elijah, Sir."

He told James he had asked the Lord, why should I go to a foreign country with people I do not even know, and God had answered him with that particular Bible verse. It served to remind him why he was there.

The chaplain had noticed his Bible had been used a lot and was curious about a hole in it. Corporal King answered, "Oh this little hole."

He proceeded to explain the event that led to the incident. He had been out on patrol and his team had gotten ambushed and one of the bullets hit the Bible that was in his left breast pocket. He had felt a sting in the area and was not aware of anything until they got back to camp. He said that the adrenalin takes over and you are not aware of anything else but to take your position and defend your unit.

His unit had lost one soldier that day. The enemy already knew they were on patrol that day and ambushed them. He said that the incident lasted for about 4 hours, and they had won that small battle that day. When he returned to camp and was taking a shower, he noticed a bruise on his left side near his heart. It was sore to touch, and he went to be checked out by medical personnel to make sure that he was okay. The medic had told him that he was lucky and asked him what in the world had stopped that bullet from penetrating his heart and killing him. He reached into his pocket and pulled out the Bible with the bullet still in it. Corporal King said, God had spared his life that day and he is reminded by this verse as to why he is here. He told God, Send me. Chaplain paused for a minute and then spoke. "God is still in the miracle business," he said, "and He is going to use you, Corporal, for something."

Corporal King told him that God was already using him. He told him that he has witnessed secretly to locals and was leading a small group that was holding meetings with four other soldiers in secret and telling them about Jesus. He had to be incredibly careful, due to the country putting restrictions on people gathering in Jesus' name. This gathering was endangering the lives of the people, but also his own and that of his friends. He told the chaplain after God had spared him that day from that bullet, he had to tell those around him that God is real and wanted him to spread the good news. Captain Robinson had asked Corporal King to see if he could attend the small group with him and his friends just one time, because he had to return to Kabul shortly. Corporal King was so excited that he ran to his friends and told them about what the chaplain had said. The following day, Captain had told his chain of command that he was attending a small coffee gathering with some locals to improve relations with the locals.

Captain had asked Corporal King's Staff Sergeant if he could take him and four other soldiers to be with him as security protection for safety reasons. Staff Sergeant agreed and they set out. They looked around the block before entering carefully into the establishment where about fourteen men, women and a few children had gathered to hear from Captain Robinson about the love of Jesus. The Chaplain opened the Bible to John 13:34. "A new command I give you: Love one another. As I have loved you, so you must love one another."

As he was about to pray for the small gathering, a small child came running into the room screaming and strapped with bombs around his chest and pulled the string that activated the detonation of the bomb. As the bomb went off, Captain was launched up against the wall and fell to the ground. As he laid there bloodied from his wounds and with ringing in his ears and being disoriented from the blast, all he could see was Corporal King dragging his bloodied body towards the chaplain with the small Bible in his right hand. He reached out to Captain Robinson and laid it in his right hand. With his last words he said, "I am sorry for bringing you here, but do not worry about me. I am going home to see Jesus."

Then he took his last breath. The sound of the blast was heard at the compound, and it was put on alert. A patrol unit was dispatched with medical personnel. The medics reached Captain Robinson and transported him immediately via helicopter to a nearby Army medical trauma center. He and some of the other survivors were stabilized. As soon as the medical team had conducted emergency surgery on the injuries that Captain Robinson had suffered and had gotten him stabilized, they transferred him to Regional Medical Center near Ramstein Air Base, Germany.

Chapter 4
Healing

Jeremiah 30:17 (NIV)
"I will restore your health, and I will heal your wounds, declares the Lord."

While in flight to Germany, Captain Robinson came in and out of consciousness. He said his wife's name - Mandy - and the staff that was attending him had told him that his wife was waiting for him in Germany. The Red Cross had contacted her and flown her to Germany.

While in flight, he had a dream in which he was standing in front of Jesus. While in his dream, Jesus had told him that his time had not come and that the harvest is plentiful, but the workers are few. "You have a lot of work ahead of you so that you can spread the good news of Jesus Christ. So, I will be with you through hard and good times. Your recovery will be hard and long, but if you hold onto my word, I will be with you to the end."

In his dream Jesus had asked him to cast his net after his recovery. Jesus told him that many will come to salvation through him and Mandy. Jesus had told him he would go to a foreign land and would have a heavy loss while there, but he would be with him, giving him strength and hope for the future.

When the plane had landed at Ramstein airfield, the staging buses were ready to transport all the injured and triage them for further treatment.

Captain Robinson had to be transported to surgery to amputate his right leg and he had lost his right eye during the blast. He had also suffered a traumatic brain injury and the doctors were worried about the swelling of his brain. In the operating room there were several medical specialists in the field of trauma. They were the best. Captain Robinson was in the operating room for about eight hours. In the meantime, Mandy was praying along with the chaplain who was assigned to the hospital. Mandy had also told everyone back home to keep praying. Finally, the head doctor approached Mandy and told her that he had pulled through, but it would be a long road to recovery. He was transferred to the ICU and was being carefully monitored by the staff. The first 48 hours would be crucial, and he needed all the attention of the nurses during this time. Mandy could not go to visit him yet, but as soon as the doctors gave the green light to see him, they would let her know.

Finally on the third day, Captain Robinson began to come around. The first thing he had asked the nurses for was his wife. Mandy came running to the room and slowly embraced him and gave him a kiss on the forehead. The first thing he told her was that he had kept the promise he had made - I came back to be by your side. She broke down in tears and thanked God for bringing him back. He was in a lot of pain and had asked the nurses for some water. He had been in a coma for quite some time and could not remember what had happened to him. He was asking for all the other Marines who had been with him. Mandy told him that most of them did not make it. He asked Mandy to pray for them and their families and they held hands and asked Almighty God for healing, comfort and strength for the families of the lost loved ones. The presence of the Holy Spirit came into that room that day. Mandy and James felt peace and knew that God was working as they prayed. James had stated that the military had lost some good men, but Heaven had gained warriors. There were tears coming out of Captain Robinson's eyes and Mandy just wiped them away with her hair.

After a few days in ICU, he then was transported to a regular room and a team of physical therapists were waiting on him and started to work on his range of motion. It was then that he had discovered that he was missing his right leg. It was a devastating blow to him, but Mandy was there to comfort and encourage him. He also came to the realization that he was missing his right eye. He felt horrible, but Jesus' presence came into the room and filled him with the Holy Spirit. He started praying and Mandy knew that something had happened when she came back to the room after getting some coffee. She did not ask anything; she just held his hand. After a few days of getting his muscles stronger, the physical therapists got him out of bed and sat him in a wheelchair and rolled him down to physical therapy to the prosthetic department to fit him for an artificial leg. One of the technicians was a non-believer. He was always asking him how he could love a God that let this happen to him. Captain Robinson had answered him, "I do not know, but I do know that he will heal me and still has a plan for me. He will not forsake me, even as I go through the valley of recovery."

He quoted Psalm 23:4 to himself: "Even though I walk through the darkest valley, I will fear no evil, for you are with me; your rod and staff, they comfort me."

He would wake up every day as he went through therapy and would quote this verse over and over. His therapy sessions were long and painful for him, but he knew he needed to go through it in order to function and be able to support himself physically. He had Mandy at his side every single day. The physical therapist who did not believe in God worked with him every day even though he tried to get out of it, because all he talked about was God. He saw the Captain in pain every single day, but he would quote Bible verses instead of cursing God. He would always praise God and hum hymns that he remembered from his youth. The physical therapist would see the joy in his face and started asking questions on how he could get some of that joy. God was working through the chaplain to shine his light to others in his dark days of recovery.

One morning the therapist came crying to the chaplain and told him that his wife was in a terrible accident in Germany. It was not her fault, but she needed prayers and Chaplain and Mandy started praying for physical healing and that God would go before her while she was in surgery and recovery. She had suffered a head injury, and doctors told the therapist that a miracle would be needed even after surgery. So, Mandy, chaplain and the therapist prayed, and the presence of the Holy Spirit was in the room and the therapist accepted Jesus that day. The therapist told the chaplain thank you and he left the room and went to be beside his wife in the intensive care unit. Two weeks passed, and the Captain had not seen his regular therapist and was asking for him. As soon as he arrived from therapy, Mandy greeted him at the door and told him, I have a surprise for you. As soon as she opened the door to his room, his therapist was standing there with his wife in a wheelchair. He wanted the chaplain to see what God had done. There was rejoicing and crying that morning.

The chaplain forgot all the pain that he had gone through in therapy that day and knew that God's hand of healing had taken place.

Well, it was time to be transferred to San Antonio to complete the therapy that he needed. Ramstein Hospital had done what they could do, but he needed further therapy and surgeries. He would also need therapy and help with his post-traumatic stress disorder. When he and Mandy arrived in San Antonio, he was then transferred to Brooke Medical Center, where he would continue his rehab. To his surprise, his mom and family were waiting for him at the hospital. They had gotten military permission to come on the base through the public relations officer. There was again joy and prayer time and praise to God for bringing Captain Robinson back home. The next day, the neurosurgeon came to talk to him about the loss of his eye and some surgery that needed to be done on his right arm. He had lost some mobility, but also had some problems holding on to a cup of coffee, but the doctor told him that he would recover.

Captain Robinson also had asked the doctor why he was having so much pain in the leg that had been amputated. The doctor called it phantom pain.

About 3 months had passed by and Mandy was staying at a lodging until they would find out what the military was going to do with the Chaplain. He told

Mandy that he would love to stay active duty, but with his current condition the military would not approve. Sure, enough the commanding officer of his unit came down and explained to him what would happen during the transitioning of his good conduct medical discharge. He would receive a medical service rating so that then he could ask the Veterans Administration for an increase in benefits to which he was entitled. The news devastated him and Mandy knew that this might spiral him into depression. As he was being discharged from the hospital, Mandy had found a church and an apartment to rent close to the VA hospital to continue to receive the care that he needed. She had also found a job to support them, while Chaplain's Robinson pay was straightened out.

Mandy had noticed that he was angry all the time and was always looking up at the trees and would always sit in a restaurant with his back to the wall. He had also started drinking alcohol even though he had never drunk alcohol before. He said it was to numb the pain. Mandy encouraged him to start attending the sessions to help him with his anger issues and depression. He always told her that he was okay and that he did not need any help. Mandy had talked to the pastor of the church she was attending and had asked for the church family to start praying for James. She knew that the devil was trying to take over his life and she prayed over him every night. She would stay up late and see him have nightmares of the incident that had happened to him in Afghanistan. He would wake up with sweat just pouring out of him and all the sheets of the bed would be soaked with his tears and sweat. Mandy at times would have to sleep on the couch, because he was so violent in his dreams.

She was really concerned about his mental health. She reached out to the chaplain on the base and sought counseling for both of them.

The chaplain on the base had referred her to the VA chaplain and he came out to visit one day. James was so upset at him being in his home that he threw him out and was upset at Mandy for not talking to him first. James would not leave the apartment and did not want to do anything. All he wanted to do was sleep and feel sorry for himself. His alcohol consumption increased, and he started taking pain pills that were prescribed by the pain management doctor. He was also starting to buy pills behind Mandy's back and began to be dependent on the pills. He had become addicted to pain pills. Mandy did not know how much more she could take of this and called his mom and family for help. She needed support spiritually and physically in dealing with a wounded soldier, who had lost his military career to an explosion. He was not even praying at this time; he had lost himself and had quit spending time with God. His family had come from out of town and had brought him a surprise. They believed that this might put him on the path to help sooth his pain. As soon as the family had walked in, they were followed by Alejandro, his old college friend.

James' eyes brightened up and he held Alejandro for a long time. They both cried and Alejandro's heart was broken, because he had seen his friend during happier times. James had changed so much that even Alejandro did not recognize him.

After talking to him for a while, he talked to Mandy. He believed that he might have a solution to all of this. He gathered James and Mandy and asked them if they could both go back to Guatemala with him. He needed help in his church and Alejandro believed that it would help James to get him out of there and breath and get some fresh air the mountains of Guatemala. James' family would pay for the trip. Mandy and James already had passports. He had gotten approved for one hundred percent service-connected disability and had filed and been approved for social security disability. So, the disability money that he was receiving would be deposited automatically at a local San Antonio bank and Mandy and him could make a living in Guatemala from it.

Chapter 5
Harvesting the Fields

Mathew 9:37 (NIV)
"Then He said to his disciples, 'The harvest is plentiful, but the workers are few.'"

Mandy, Alejandro, and James were back together as the three amigos. The Bible says that when two or three are gathered in my name, I am with them. So, before they boarded the aircraft at the San Antonio International Airport, they prayed for God's anointing on the trip and God's hedge of protection – that He would give wisdom and help those in need of hope. While in flight to Guatemala City, Pastor James told Alejandro that he had done some research on the poverty of Guatemala. According to the World Bank, Guatemala is listed as the 10th country with a 59.30% poverty rate in the world. Guatemala is used as a route for sex traffickers. 96 percent of victims are from other southern countries that are transported through Guatemala. The other 4 percent are the women and children of Guatemala; this is due to poverty and domestic abuse. Pastor Alejandro told Mandy and James that he needed help to reach out and educate the abused women and children in the compound that his town had built. He had a program for those that were recovering from addiction to cocaine and other drugs.

They also had some farmland donated by a local to be used in the growing of their own food. Some chickens, cows, and goats were being raised on the farm to provide food and milk for the area. Alejandro said that he was always being threatened by gang members and drug lords in the area to cease and desist his programs. He always woke up in prayer and asking God to protect him with His right hand and surround all the people involved in this ministry. He called his project Proyecto de Esperanza. James and Mandy smiled and said that they liked the name, Project of Hope. After about 3 hours of flight, they landed in Guatemala City and went through customs and showed their passports and work permits, which were required while they were in Guatemala. Mandy and James were fluent in reading, speaking, and writing the Spanish language. The three of them took a taxi to the bus station that would take them to Asuncion Mita which is name of the town that Alejandro had set up camp for helping other villages and cities in the surrounding area. The bus trip took about 3 hours. The smell of the chickens and men that do not use deodorant made Mandy and James' face turn green. Alejandro just laughed; he was used to the odor. Thankfully, Mandy had a small bottle of anointing oil with her with the smell of frankincense and myrrh and coated the bottom of her nostrils, which drowned some of the mixed odors from the bus. There were a few rest stops that the bus would stop at so that people could get a snack or use the bathroom. These routes were set up by the bus company to make money along the way for long trip passengers. Alejandro introduced new foods to James and Mandy along the way. They had some carne asada tacos mixed with onion, cilantro, and curtido, which is cabbage-soaked in liquid spices. James said they were delicious. After the rest and filling their bellies off they went to continue the trip to Alejandro's town. It was nightfall when they got in and all that the trip adventurers wanted to do was go to sleep. Alejandro's family was so happy to receive them and all they wanted to do was talk and get to meet the newcomers to town. It was an event for the people to see Americans come to town. Alejandro told his family that they would talk in the morning, because they were so tired from the long trip.

James and Mandy were woken up by the rooster crowing in the morning right outside their window. James said that the rooster would be a good fried at this time and Mandy bumped him with her elbow. So, they got freshened up and were guided to the smell of coffee and a wonderfully cooked breakfast of huevos rancheros, refried beans, and tortillas with queso blanco (white cheese). Mandy commented on the freshness of the coffee and how sweet it was. You did not have add any sugar to it. It was so delicious that she had three cups of it. James also made a statement about it, and he just wanted to add milk to it. The milk came from the cows that the community farm had. After eating with the family, they all gathered on the porch that overlooked a small valley. They introduced themselves in Spanish and all were amazed at how fluent they both spoke. They laughed and finally Alejandro prayed over James and Mandy and the task at hand. They all sought wisdom and guidance on what God had in store and remembered Psalm 119:105 - "Thy word is a lamp unto my feet, and a light unto my path."

Bellies full again, Alejandro took them and showed them the campus that had been enclosed with a mural protecting the chapel and the school campus for educating children that were picked off the streets, because they had been abandoned by their families. He had to protect the children due to the frequent kidnapping of young boys and girls that were used in sexual exploitation. Also, it protected frequent vandalism and reoccurring property thefts from local gangs. The camp was also used by American doctors and nurses that would provide medical care or minor surgery on patients. People would walk for many miles and even days to come to this event held every quarter and would camp out over night at the gates of the campus. There would be sickness of all kinds and some needed spiritual help because it was the last place that they would see due to their untreated illness. Mandy and James got to work in helping to guide women and children to the proper team. They would pray with everyone that came in and then leave them in the hands of the medical staff. There were hundreds of people waiting to be seen and not all could be seen in one day.

The gates would open at five in the morning and close at nine at night so that the staff could get some rest. It was so sad to see people still waiting at the gates even as they closed. Alejandro would try to provide food and water for the people outside the gates but did not have enough. It broke James and Mandy's hearts to see this firsthand. The need was so great in different areas of the campus. James prayed and immediately thought about his military friends and had reached out to see if they could provide aid in food, water, and needed medical supplies. About two months later, three heavy duty trucks were honking at the community gate filled with supplies. Alejandro, Mandy, and James began to cry and praise God for all the supplies that were lifted to the throne of grace. The whole community helped to unload the trucks and sang songs of worship and praise, thanking God for the miracle that He provided. You see God listens to your prayers and you must have faith and stand firm on the word of God. After 2 weeks of the medical team taking care of as many people as they could, not all could be seen or treated. As the end of the time was quickly approaching people would try to cut the line and use force to get in to be seen. It got so violent at one point that they had to close the gates and call the local police department to disperse the angry folks. Mostly it was gang members trying to instigate trouble. They did not like the medical team being there, because it was hurting the revenue from selling coca leaves. The locals and other villagers from far away would chew on the leaves to relieve hunger and fatigue, due to long travels. James noticed that and one day he left the compound to investigate this coca leaves effect. James had gone through drug rehab and had left San Antonio to leave all of that behind. He left the compound without telling his wife or Alejandro. That was not good, because 1 Peter 5:8 tells us that the enemy the devil prowls around like a roaring lion, looking for someone to devour. James had let his guard down and some of the people in line were offering some of the coca leaves to chew on and he complied. He spoke fluent Spanish and he was laughing and talking to the locals.

At times he did not make any sense, because coca leaves tend to increase brain activity and have numbing, anesthetic effects which can lead to addiction due to the content of cocaine found in the leaves. So, James was hooked on drugs again and had been caught in with the wrong people. The addiction got worse, and he started owing money to them. The group would send a couple of young men to request money from James and he could not provide it. They started harassing him and beat him up one time and as he returned to the compound Alejandro and Mandy noticed him and attended to his wounds and he explained to them that he was in serious trouble and that next time the gang would take some fingers from him until they got their money. Alejandro asked him how much he owed. He said over thirty thousand dollars already and interest was being accrued according to the gang. Alejandro told him that he could not raise that kind of money. He was so disappointed in James and told him to stay in the compound and be under watch to try to help him recover from the addiction.

Mandy spent hours seeing James's shake from the withdrawals. He was under a watchful eye even from the workers in the compound.

They prayed around the clock for James to recover from his addiction. Time passed and James was feeling better. Mandy decided it was time to go to the market with the other women to buy provisions. The compound had a van and would take them to the center of town and dropped them off at the marketplace. There were about seven women assigned with the task of getting all the items needed to feed the women and children. As the women were walking down a narrow street, a black SUV pulled up and took Mandy. The other ladies tried to help Mandy, but the men were so powerful and pointed the guns at them and the women could not save her. They called the local police, but they were under the payroll of the gang. So, they really did not help much and pretended that they were going to get Mandy back. The van came back to pick up the women who were crying.

Alejandro was driving the van and they told him that the gang had kidnaped Mandy. He told the women not to tell James what had happened until he consulted with the local authorities.

He dropped the ladies off and went directly to the comandancia (police precinct.) He went to speak to the chief of police, and he told him that he had some men already looking for her. The chief told Alejandro that they would not find Mandy. After talking to the chief, he drove back to the compound and proceeded to let James know what had happened. James went hysterical and started to scream and shout and blamed himself for the kidnapping of his wife. About two days passed with no word about Mandy, but then on the third day a ten-year-old child came to the gate asking for the American. James came to the gate and little Carlito told him that the men that had his wife were going to do something drastic to her if James did not pay the ransom. They remembered Matthew 18:20 - "For where two or three are gathered in my name, there am I with them."

A lot of the Hispanic community and even those that he helped daily surrounded him. They were speaking in tongues, and the presence of the Holy Spirit filled the room. They raised Mandy's name to the throne of grace and mercy. James and Alejandro were prostrating themselves. The community had even fasted from the time that Mandy went missing.

By six o'clock that evening, they heard a loud screeching of tires, and they ran out to towards the gate that was locked, Alejandro was ahead of them and as he opened the gate, he saw Mandy's body lying on the pavement. She was motionless and not breathing. The gang had put a bullet to her head and around her neck was a note attached that read, "Where is your God now?"

Permit me to pause for a moment and put in here my personal view on God when we are going through tribulations. First of all, God is love. God loves you and He will never forsake you, even in hard times. The devil will use these thoughts in your mind that there is no God or why did God let this happen?

Things might be so difficult for us to understand, God is working it out, He is there beside you. God loves you and all He wants to show His loving purpose for your life. God is weaving or mending the torn threads in our lives; that includes the suffering, heartaches and even our mistakes and turning them into a beautiful tapestry. So, even in your mistakes or terrible circumstances that happen in your life, you can trust God. He is ever present and will be with you to the end. Your walk with Jesus will never be without troubles, tears, sadness, broken relations, disappointments, but what distinguishes your walk is your relationship with Jesus. Keep trusting, hoping, worshipping, and praising God despite all your troubles. You see even through our hard times we can find grace, the unmerited favor of God towards us. Thank you for giving me a minute, and now back to the story.

When James got to her body, all he could do was hold her and say I am sorry. He did not blame God for this. He felt it was his fault that all of this had happened, and he picked up her body and carried her into their room and closed the door behind him.

The next morning, Alejandro knocked at the door and wanted to express the sadness that he and the whole community were sharing with James. He asked James to go back to America and that he would raise enough money to transport him and her back home. He asked James to seek medical help for his addiction and depression. Alejandro could not help him in that matter, but all he could do was provide spiritual support and comfort for his friend. He called her parents in Colorado, and they wanted to have Mandy buried in a plot that they had bought for the whole family. James agreed and said farewell to Alejandro and his new friends in Guatemala. So, the next day, he took a flight back to America and flew into Denver.

The family was waiting for him at the airport, but they were mad at him for the loss of their loved one. Mandy was a special girl to the whole family. She wanted to change the world through Jesus. After the funeral was over, Mandy's family had asked him to leave, and they did not want to hear or see from him ever again. James then set his sights on going back to San Antonio to be admitted into a recovery program at a VA facility and for treatment for the depression that he was experiencing.

Chapter 6
I Will Not Leave You

Deuteronomy 31:8 (NIV)
"The Lord himself goes before you and will be with you; He will never leave you nor forsake you. Do not be afraid; do not be dismayed."

James came through the emergency room at the local VA hospital and told the doctor that he was addicted to pain pills and wanted to take his life. He was going down a dark path and needed help. The doctor took some blood samples and a urine sample, and they showed that James tested positive for oxycodone. The doctor came into his room and told him that they were going to get him a room in the mental health ward. He asked if he was willing to spend about 3 months in receiving therapy. He of course agreed to be helped. He was at the end of his rope and wanted help. He had not slept for quite some time and was falling asleep standing up. The doctor had requested some help for him to be escorted to the mental health unit and to be under watch for a few days. He did not want to eat or drink anything, so the doctor ordered him to have an intravenous drip to try to put some electrolytes in him. He finally fell asleep, and he slept for 2 days and of course was being monitored to make sure that he was still breathing. When he finally woke up and freshened up, he was slowly gaining some energy and started talking to the staff.

The nurse took his IV out and encouraged him to have some water and Jell-O to start off. He took his time eating, but he managed to get some down. The next day he had an appointment with his psychiatrist who would guide and treat him as he recovered from drug addiction. He was also under a watch for a few days, just to help prevent him from taking his life. During the first visit, James did not say much, because he was still grieving from the loss of his wife. As he left the office, he wanted to go back to his room, but the staff told him that he needed to go to group session and meet other veterans who were experiencing drug dependency. All the veterans that were there were a variety of ages, and there was a total of six in his group. There were even three veterans from the Vietnam War that were still seeking medical therapy, due to the lasting effects of Post Traumatic Stress Disorder. They had been in therapy before, but they would always come back to seek help and to be able to help other younger veterans in the process. Mike served as a Marine in Vietnam from 1965 to 1968. He was always dealing with painful memories from the war and tried to hide it from his wife and family.

Always avoiding the topic of war, he would push it off and hide his time in the service from friends and people whom he encountered. He had marital issues, depression and his PTSD got worse. He finally realized that a Marine veteran can always reach out for help and support no matter how long it had been since your military service ended. He came to the VA because he felt comradery in sharing stories with other Vietnam veterans. Mike made a statement; we were in different times, different wars, but we all end up with the same feelings that are not easy to shake off. We share the same trauma and that brings us all together to share and heal.

Ralph, an Air Force veteran, shared his story. He had been working on a security post when the Tet offensive surprise attack conducted by the Vietcong and the North Vietnamese Army began. He saw horrific things happening in sequence. When he returned home, he like many other soldiers did not experience a warm welcome. Ralph tried to put all these experiences behind and move on but could not.

Ralph said that he turned to a life of violence, took a lot of drugs, was a cocaine addict, partied and lived a life that he did not care what would happen to him. He took odd jobs as a door attendant, bouncer and would brawl with anyone who would look at him. He even showed his dentures to the group, because he had lost so many teeth along the way in fighting. One night, he took such a massive overdose that he felt that his heart was jumping out of his body. He said that night he cried out in what seemed to be a prayer to live. He woke up the next day and never touched drugs again. He asked God to guide him to other believers in Christ so that he could grow closer to Jesus. He became a pastor and helped many come to Christ. He always gives his testimony on how God reached down and saved him that night. Ralph talked about losing some battle buddies to drug overdose and suicide. Today, he still struggles with temptations to be lured into drugs, and that is why he continues to attend meetings at the VA center.

He is encouraged by other fellow veterans in the

group and always closes the group in prayer. Many Vietnam Veterans have a bond, fighting together and returning home to build their lives with families and communities in our nation. Many still face challenges and their stories of trauma are still embedded in their minds. Some seek help and support through different programs available to them. Mike and Ralph, like many other veterans, have sought God and share their stories about how Jesus has transformed their lives. There is great power in a story that you tell, and it can transform the world around you.

Carlos, an Army veteran served as a medic in Afghanistan, and was injured and evacuated to Germany and eventually medically retired. He explained how he lost sleep, had flashbacks, and suffered the effects in being overmedicated, which led to drug dependency. He told the group that his wife Ligia was a big support in his life. He tried to find an outlet by writing a book to focus his energy and keep his mind occupied. He stated that it is a journey to be taken with other veterans that suffer from PTSD and you should never walk or feel alone.

Carlos found ways to help other veterans along the way by setting up community events for them and passing out information on PTSD awareness and found the Lord to sustain him in hard times. The clinician had talked to Carlos to see if he could start talking to James and try to engage him in the group. After the group therapy session, Carlos managed to start a conversation with James and after several times having coffee together in the cafeteria, James began to talk to Carlos and explained what had happened to his wife in Guatemala. Carlos told James, the light of Jesus lives in you and that the light will overcome any darkness in you. The light guided by the Holy Spirit shines in you if you pray and seek His word daily. The more you seek God, the brighter the light becomes and wherever you go, you bring a light greater than any darkness that surrounds you. Carlos stopped the conversation and began to pray for James a prayer like this: Lord God, the Bible says that the Lord gives strength to his children. The Lord blesses His people with peace. I pray for peace to come back into James' life.

Help him to get through the valley of pain, depression, sadness, guiltiness and restore peace and joy in his life that only You can do and rekindle his light to shine brighter every single day. May he be a lighthouse and shine to those that surround him that live in darkness. In the name of Jesus, we pray. Amen. That night, James finally got some rest. Carlos and James became good friends, and they drank a lot of coffee and shared many stories.

The next day after he had met with his psychiatrist, he went to attend group and there was a young man, in his early thirties. His name was Joe. He served in the Marine Corps in Iraq at the beginning of the invasion. Joe said that he saw a lot of death, from the enemy's side and some Marines who died and were his friends. He said that transitioning out of the Marines was so hard, because he went from high adrenalin all the time to being at home where everything was normal. Joe could not sleep because of nightmares and anxiety attacks and started to look to alcohol for a way out.

He became homeless and was always thinking about committing suicide and refused help, because he thought a man should never reach out for help, and he had to deal with his own problems. One day as he was on the street, a young Christian lady reached out and brought him some food and saw beyond the filth and how awful Joe smelled.

She saw a man that God had created in His own image and just needed some polishing. Joe said that she is now his wife and completely changed his life. She encouraged him to talk about what was going on inside his head. He attended church and found a group of other wounded veterans. Joe encourages other veterans to find a therapy group and he knows that you can succeed and overcome any obstacle. Joe did make a statement that resounded in the group. Some veterans find it hard to go to the VA, because you are treated as a number not as a person. He felt that those dealing with PTSD and mental health problems do not want the weight of the bureaucratic issues that are in the system. So, veterans should look out for other veterans who are hurting.

Weeks had passed and finally James was talking to his physician and started to open up more in the group. He told his story of what happened to him in Afghanistan and how he got hooked on pain pills. He told his story and how his addiction had led to the death of his wife. There was silence in the room that day, and then all the group gathered around James and started to pray for healing in his life.

Carlos came to James and told him the news that he was being discharged and that he would continue to pray for healing and for James to get back in the saddle and start preaching again. That is what James started to do and he went to ask the chaplain of the VA if he could volunteer and help in the hospital. The chaplain said that he would appreciate the help but would have to talk to his doctor to see if he was ready to help with the duties of a chaplain. The chaplain admired James for the enthusiasm and energy that he was displaying. James had told him that the Holy Spirit had renewed his fire to serve God and wanted to help other veterans.

Chapter 7
Let Your Light Shine

Matthew 5:16 (NIV)
"In the same way, let your light shine before others, that they may see your good deeds and glorify your Father in heaven."

James had completed his treatment for PTSD and for drug dependency and was very eager to start helping other veterans in the hospital and in the surrounding satellite clinics. He would walk the hospital halls and talk to veterans in the cafeteria. Every Thursday, there would be a man with his karaoke machine set up in the cafeteria who would start singing. He would have a line of veterans eager to sing. Some could not carry a tune in a bucket, but it was all in fun. James would laugh at some of them - quietly of course. He would ask the man for the microphone to tell all the veterans who he was and that he was available at any time to talk or just drink coffee. He would assist veterans in wheelchairs and wheel them to their appointments when other volunteers were attending to other veterans. At times he would have to rest due to his leg that had been amputated that still bothered him from time to time and it would slow him down a bit. His role as a volunteer chaplain would be of listening to the veteran and family members and provide spiritual support by prayer and he would always encourage them by quoting Joshua 1:9 "Have I not commanded you? Be strong and courageous. Do not be afraid; do not be discouraged, for the Lord your God will be with you wherever you go."

Every morning, he would sit down with veterans in the coffee shop or the waiting rooms while waiting for their appointments. He would communicate between the care team and the patient for concerns regarding their care, but most important to him was to honor the work of every veteran on what he or she had done for their country. He would visit patients that were terminal and provide help with decision making. He would talk about Jesus and what He does when you invite Him into your life. Some believed and some did not, but those that he did reach were at peace in whatever came their way. He was on call 24 hours a day, seven days a week, especially in urgent situations that came through the emergency room or wards in the hospital. He would make rounds around the chapel area and if anybody was in there, he would come up beside them and pray and just listen. One morning he was called down to the emergency room with urgency.

As he made his way down the elevator, he encountered a beautiful physician assistant and they instantly zinged, get it. They just stared for a moment, and as she was getting off the elevator, he saw her last name and the oncology department on her name tag and made a note to himself to follow up on her. When he reached his destination, he asked one of the staff members who had paged him and immediately a doctor approached him and told him at the request of the patient's wife, he was paged. As he pulled the curtains back the body was covered, and the patient's wife told him that it was Carlos, his friend that went through the program with him. He was devastated to see him lifeless and started sobbing. He had to gather his composure and provide support for his wife. They both held on to each other with grief. He could not believe what had taken place and soon he asked what had happened. Ligia started to tell him about what he was going through. He started to go into stages that he would be talking to her and suddenly he would be in a state of a trance, like if he were back in Afghanistan and screaming aloud to other imaginary soldiers that were with him and would give orders on how to help him with assisting wounded soldiers. He would cry for those that he could not save over and over. He would also quote a verse in his sleep as he prayed for the dead: Revelation 21:4 "He will wipe every tear from their eyes. There will be no more death, or mourning or crying or pain, for the old order of things have passed away."

He would come out of his trance and tell Ligia that he did not do enough for them. Ligia would call their local pastor, and the community group of the church would gather around and pray for Ligia and Carlos. She thought he was getting better, but one day while she went shopping, she came back with a handful of groceries into the house and called his name, but he did not answer. She was calling for him repeatedly and at one point started to call him lazy and went storming into the small office he had for projects on which he was working. She found him and she went to grab him by the shoulder and his body just slumped over. He had acquired a gun from the street. She had Carlos' body transported here and then the local authorities would transport the body to the coroner. She asked James if he would provide his services for the funeral, and he agreed instantly.

After the funeral had passed by, he told Ligia to follow up in grief counseling with her pastor or to call him when she needed too. He hugged her and said goodbye for now.

As he started his Monday routine, he recalled the physician assistant that he had seen on the elevator and was on a mission to find her and treat her to a cup of coffee. He went to the oncology department and went to each patient that was there to see a doctor or to be treated for their diagnosis. You could see new veterans and their spouses when they were there to receive the bad word called cancer. You could see the faces of despair, but Chaplain James would always ask to see if he could pray with them. He would pray this with each family and also asked if he could anoint the member with oil. Jesus' light was shining in James again. The spiritual fire had reignited in him.

(Lord, help me to hear your voice in the middle of this valley that I am going through. Lord, your word says, you are the hope for the hopeless, so I am running to you with both hands stretched out and grabbing unto to You. Renew my spirit and heal me. Refill my cup with hope and remind me that hope is unbreakable. In Jesus' name. Amen.) He would always carry a box of tissues, because after he prayed there would be tears and the peace of the Holy Spirit would fill the room. As he departed, he would give a little card with the following verse: Isaiah 40:31 "But those who hope in the LORD will renew their strength. They will soar on wings like eagles; they will run and not grow weary; they will walk and not be faint."

After he had prayed with the families in the room, he went to the front desk and asked for a physician assistant with the last name Friedman, (he had researched the last name, and it stands for follower of peace.) The clerk at the front desk told him that he had to have an appointment to see her, and he told the clerk that he was one of the volunteer chaplains on staff, but she insisted that he needed an appointment. So, he asked to see if he could leave her a message and the clerk complied. He had given her his extension number and asked to talk to her when she had a break or lunchtime. He left the clinic and started to proceed to visit the wards at the hospital. When he had completed his rounds the chaplain's secretary gave him a message. He opened the note that read: I eat lunch at 1300 at the cafeteria. It was from Ms. Gracie Friedman. He was so excited that he yelled hallelujah in the office, and everybody came in running thinking that he had gotten hurt. He told them that he was thankful and praising God. They all laughed and left his office. The next day, he was early in the cafeteria and was waiting anxiously, feeling like his heart was about to come out of his chest. He was really nervous. As she entered the cafeteria, he thought he had seen an angel just floating on a cloud and he could not take his eyes off her.

When she finally recognized him and asked him how his day was going, all he could do was babble. She laughed and finally he gathered his composure. He introduced himself even though she already knew his name and what he did in the hospital. She had done her homework on the chaplain. He asked her if he could treat her for lunch. She of course said yes and said she never turned down a free meal. Gracie saw beyond his scars and saw a man after God's own heart. So, each ordered a cheeseburger and fries. James had asked for ranch dressings to dip his fries in, and Gracie said you better order extra ranch dressing. They both liked dipping their fries in ranch dressing. As they both sat down, they could not take their eyes off each other. So needless to say, they did not eat, and time went by so fast. She had to get back to work and take care of patients. James was very bold and asked her if she would go on a date with him. She of course agreed and said that she loved Mexican food.

Friday came and after work James went to pick her up and they went to a good Mexican restaurant, and she had ordered guacamole and white cheese dip for her chips. They ordered a fajita plate for two with chicken, meat, and shrimp with rice and beans. She said the reason she likes this food is because you can smell an aroma that makes you want to eat a lot. They both laughed. Time went by so quickly, but again they would just stare at each other as if they had known each other for a very long time. After eating a good meal, he took her to a safe and wonderful park and they both sat on a kids' swing and started talking about each other. Gracie was a Christian and James loved that she loved the Lord with all her heart. Again, God had blessed him with a God-fearing woman. When he walked her back to his apartment and was about to give her a kiss on the cheek, she grabbed him and laid a good smacker on him. He had to come up for air and she bid him good night. As he was going back to his car, he stared singing a song by Chris Tomlin, "Good, Good Father."

They had been dating for quite some time and James had asked her to marry him and she said yes.

She moved into James apartment because it was slightly bigger than hers. Every morning, they would both wake up and spend time in prayer and reading God's word. They would pray for wisdom and discernment with all the decisions that were to make that day with their lives and the lives of those whom they came in contact with. He would always ask God to light their light so that they could shine in somebody's life every single day. As he went in to work, he would always invite veterans to come and hear his sermon. He would set aside 30 minutes of preaching. Staff members, patients and veterans that had appointments would come to hear him. He noticed an elderly man that came in every day and would never miss a sermon. He wondered if he had to see a doctor every day. As he made his way to meet him and asked him for his name, the man said that his name was Chip. James asked him to have coffee with him and he obliged.

As they sat, James asked him why he was here every day. Chip said that he was alone, and his wife had passed away. He felt very lonely and that coming to the VA, he is able to talk to young and old veterans and share their stories. He told James that he had heard a lot of stories and that he could write a book on them, but he sighed, I am too old and have a terrible memory. James told him that they could both sit down for coffee anytime and that made Chip glad. Months had gone by, and James' life was a happy one with Gracie by his side. As they were having dinner one night, his cell phone rang, and it was his mother asking to see if he could return home. His dad had had a stroke, and it would be a long recovery and he would probably not be able to preach anymore. That night it was quiet in James' apartment. Gracie and James immediately prayed for guidance in this matter. The next morning Gracie got up and told James that they had to move and help his family in Montana. Both of them had had a hard time sleeping that night. She went to work that day and put her notice in and told her boss that she was heading to Montana.

The boss told her to try to find a VA facility and get state certified so that she could continue to practice her medical skills. James went and told the senior chaplain that he had received a call from his mom, and he told him to go and see what God is going to do in his life. It looked as if it were a new beginning, a new chapter, new path, a new direction where God is going to provide the wind on your sails. Both chaplains prayed and there was peace in James' decision. So, they had a moving company move all their items and Gracie sold her car and off they went to Montana.

I would like to close this chapter and talk to my fellow veterans - especially those who have been diagnosed with post-traumatic stress disorder. There is a saying that says that time will heal all wounds. Those wounds can't be healed if you don't seek help to close that wound. Please find a path to gather with other men and women who have walked in one way or another in a trauma related event. You will gather with them and hear their stories that led to their depression, anxiety, anger, feeling alone, guilt, and pain. When you put words that are related to these things into action, then you start a process towards healing. The hardest part of recovery is that you have to fight against feelings of weakness, against your military training, against those memories that remind you of those who have fallen, your fellow warriors. All these points can lead to isolation and the results can be devastating if you ignore it. Whether it was a paramedic, fire fighter, police officer, nurse, doctor or any person that has been exposed to some kind of trauma to trigger PTSD, there is help. Healing is a choice, and it is up to you. Pursue healing.

Chapter 8
Returning Home

Matthew 12:44 (NIV)
"Then it says, 'I will return to my house from which I came'; and when it comes, it finds it unoccupied, swept, and put in order."

Before you as the reader start reading this chapter, may I intervene just for a little. When I was younger, I could drive for a total of fourteen to sixteen hours one way to my long destinations. My personal experience was to drive with the whole family and if it was up to me back then, just stop for a quick tinkle. My boys would want me to stop at everything that looked so cool to them, but no, we have no time for that, we must get to our destination. Of course, we would stop to eat, and I would tell them to hurry up so that we can get back on the road and reach our destination. Now, I don't know about you, but I would always look for a sign and see how much closer we were getting to our destination. With all of my rush to get there, I would not even pay attention to all that God had created for me. Finally, when we got to our destination, I would be so tired that I would sleep for a very long time and the kids were ready to go and have fun, but I was too tired. So, I would miss a day and rest while my family went out to have fun. What I am trying to say is slow down and enjoy the beauty that God created for you. Slow down to have fun with your family, listen to them, laugh with them and take as many breaks as possible to get to your destination. Slow down to listen to God's whisper in your ear as He says, I created all of this for you to enjoy. Now, as I am older, I am not able to drive long distances and enjoy what God created for me. If I do drive, what used to take fourteen to sixteen hours, now takes two or three days. So that noise of kids in the back seat is not there anymore. As I continue to write this chapter, put your seat belt on and enjoy the scenery. Enjoy the time with family, don't be like me and hurry to get there and watch for every sign to get to your destination. Pay attention to the sign that God has blessed you, your family. May God give you and bless you with many family trips in your horizon.

The driving distance from San Antonio to Missoula, Montana was 27 hours away for a total of 1,813 miles. Before they left, they prayed a prayer of protection: Dear Heavenly Father, we pray for our trip going home. Please cover us with the blood of Jesus Christ. Protect us from any harm. May this trip be full of memories that will last a lifetime. May we see what You created for us to see and may we give You all the glory. May we be a light to those we come in contact with and reach someone for Christ. In Jesus name. Amen. He wanted to take the drive home in two days just so that he could get some rest due to his injuries that he had from the incident in Afghanistan. He suffered from chronic pain all over his body and Gracie told him that it was going to be fun and let us take in the scenery on the way there. So, the first stop going north for them would be Denver, Colorado, where they would rest. It is halfway from his destination and Gracie was just taking the wind through her hair and listening to K-Love on the radio. Gracie had never left Texas; she was born and raised in San Antonio, attended college at Texas University and after college got a job at San Antonio VA Medical Center.

It was breezy and James wanted to conserve some fuel by not using the air conditioning. They would look at each other and just say that they loved each other. James silently was thanking God for Gracie. So, their journey began going north towards San Angelo, Texas and they hoped to reach Denver, Colorado in thirteen to fifteen hours of driving. That is where they would stay the night, eat and rest and then continue the rest of the drive to Missoula, Montana. After passing San Angelo, they would head North towards, Lubbock, then towards Dumas, where they would head east towards Pueblo, Colorado. The weather was overall good except for some passing thunderstorms that they had to go through. After passing Pueblo, the next city would be Colorado Springs, Castle Rock and then Denver. They had stopped at a few rests stops and taken a stretch, but overall, the ride was comfortable. What was interesting to them was seeing different license plates from different states and to see truckers going by and some others resting at rest stops to get some shut eye. They said to each other, "I am so glad that we have truckers to deliver goods all over the country."

Thank you, truckers.

Before they were getting into the car, they both prayed with a man who was driving an eighteen-wheeler. They prayed for all truckers' families who are waiting on their loved ones while making America great. In the middle of praying, people started gathering in the group and started singing and praising God for all that He had done in their lives. Some cried and James and Gracie had met new friends. After a small conversation each family started to proceed to their destinations. James and Gracie were so happy that they had made a stop. You never know how God will use you and the people you touch along your trip. Matthew 5:13-16 tells us that we are the salt of the earth and light of the world. So, they were approaching Denver and were searching for a place to rest and find some good food. After checking into a hotel, they found a place to eat. They had filled their tummies, and it was time to go to bed. By this time James was in a lot of pain from the trip and needed the rest. As soon as showers were taken, they both fell asleep. The alarm was set for six in the morning. During the night, Gracie was awakened by James having nightmares and screaming for Corporal King.

Gracie would wake him up and ask him, who was Corporal King and he showed her the Bible that he carries and explained the story behind him receiving the Bible from Corporal King. Gracie wrapped her arms around him and all he could do was sob. He then fell back to sleep and the alarm went off at six am. They gathered all their belongings and went to eat a good breakfast with a lot of coffee. They departed Denver and proceeded towards Cheyenne, Wyoming and then north to Casper. While driving north of Casper on I-25 and then turning into I-90 West, in between Sheridan and Ranchester, they came upon a horrible wreck. There were multiple vehicles involved and no emergency crews to be found. James and Gracie parked their vehicle safely and proceeded to help the injured. Other drivers had stopped to help, and they stated that 911 had been called and emergency responders were in route. Gracie as a physician assistant was rendering first aid. Gracie told James what to do in applying any compress that he could find and hoped to stop some of the bleeding in some of the injured. Gracie was also telling some of the other drivers how to apply pressure on some of the injured.

There was a young active-duty man that was trapped in his vehicle and was not looking good. He had lost a lot of blood from the windshield being shattered and he had gone under a truck. James told him who he was and immediately they both prayed the prayer of salvation. Upon finishing the prayer, the young man passed away. James closed his eyes and covered him with a towel that he had found in the young man's car. As he was finishing with the young man, he heard Spanish voices screaming for help. It was a van full of young women and he pried the door open and started talking Spanish to them and helped them get out of the van. The driver did not make it. There were about fifteen young women compacted in this vehicle. Some had suffered severe injuries, and as he helped each one get to the side of the road where it was safe, he asked in Spanish where they were from. Some of the women had been trafficked from Honduras, Nicaragua, Guatemala, and Mexico. They were young and were being used in sex trafficking.

They were scared and did not trust anybody, not even James. He reassured them that he would not leave their side and would protect them from any harm. James was calling out for Gracie to come help these young ladies and as soon as she was free, she came over and checked the wounds of the young ladies. Speaking Spanish, James, explained to the young ladies who she was and that she was going to help as much as she could until helped arrived. State troopers had arrived first, and they had passed on the information to other emergency vehicles. Finally, the calvary had arrived - several fire trucks and some ambulances. The fire chief had to radio in some more ambulances as well as a helicopter to take the severely injured. One of the Hispanic women came to James and told him that a girl needed help really bad. She was pregnant and was worried about the unborn child. James came up to her and she had suffered a head injury as well as a broken leg. She told James in Spanish that she was having a hard time breathing, because she had been tossed out of the van. James called one of the paramedics to take a look at her.

The paramedic pulled James to the side and told him that she had suffered severe internal injuries and would probably not make it in time to a hospital. James went back to the lady and explained to her why she was having a hard time breathing. The paramedic had given her a portable oxygen tank and had wrapped her wounds and did the best he could for her. James then sat down by her side and started praying and also told her that she would be okay. He prayed with her and held her small hand and she breathed her last upon the completion of the prayer. He covered her body and then proceeded to help the rest of the Hispanic women get on board a bus that was being used to transport the walking injured. It took several hours for the area to be cleaned up and the highway to be reopened. Gracie and James were so tired and sat down by the highway in a safe place away from the traffic. A state trooper stayed behind with them and all three of them prayed and after a while of spending time with God and thanking Him for having an opportunity in sharing the gospel to those who were injured and those new friends that they had met while helping.

God has a tendency to use situations that you and I can't understand, but He has a purpose to use us to be a witness in any situation if you choose to obey Him. James and Gracie took this tragic situation and touched peoples' lives. It was late and the state trooper told them that it would take another six hours to get to Missoula and he recommended that they stay in the town of Ranchester and then proceed on to their final destination. So that is what they did, and James called his mom and explained what had happened. She told James that his dad was hanging in there, but he needed to get there as quickly as possible. So early in the morning they departed towards Missoula and drove straight to the hospital where the whole family was waiting on James. He introduced Gracie to the whole family. James and his Mom separated themselves from the family and went into the room. She told James that his Dad had been unresponsive for a long time. So, James leaned into his father's face and kissed his cheek while tears were pouring down. James said with a low voice, Dad, do you remember the verse that you used to quote to me when I was scared of the dark and could not sleep?

James opened up his Bible to Psalm 4:8 "In peace I will lie down and sleep, for you alone, LORD, make me dwell in safety."

Remember that, Dad? As soon as he said that James' Dad opened his eyes and saw James and it brought a smile on his face. A tear fell down his cheek and then he was gone to be with the Lord. His Mom told James that he was waiting on you and to see you one last time. James fell across the bed and started to sob like a baby and was apologizing for not being there to visit. He was too busy with his life and had forgotten all about his family. Listen: one day we will be in heaven with a big family and spend the rest of eternity with our brothers and sisters glorifying our Heavenly Father, but until then spend time with family. I don't want you to regret and be like James, who saw his Dad slip away and will always have that picture of saying goodbye to his Dad.

As I conclude this chapter, I will pause and say this. As a Dad myself, I have not been perfect and have many faults, but I have asked for forgiveness and always ask God to show me how to be a better husband, father, and grandfather and how to be a bold and better witness about God's glory and all the mercy that He has given me. My closing prayer is this: Almighty God, I thank You for being in my life and showing me the path that I should walk. Help me and guide me as You provide the light unto my feet. Set me on fire to seek You and spread the good news daily. May my family and friends see Jesus in and through me. In Jesus name. Amen.

Chapter 9
Walking Through the Valley

Psalm 62:6-8 (NIV)
"He alone is my rock, and my salvation, he is my fortress, I will not be shaken. My salvation and my honor depend on God; he is my mighty rock, my refuge. Trust in him at all times, O people; pour out your hearts to him, for God is our refuge."

It was October and the leaves were changing to beautiful colors, the procession was long with a lot of old friends, and all the family there at the cemetery to bid farewell to Pastor Rick Robinson. The inscription on the headstone read: "Here lies a man that followed the light of Jesus." John 8:12.

After the funeral was over, all the folks gathered at the church to celebrate the pastor's life. There was a lot of food and there was plenty of help from the congregation. After all the folks had left, some of the elders of the church approached James and wanted to set up a meeting with him to discuss plans for the church. James told them to give him a few days to gather with family and then he would come. They all agreed. James and Gracie were staying with his mom in his old high school bedroom. It had not been touched at all. The room was clean, and all his high school trophies and achievements were hanging on the wall. Gracie just chuckled and said that she had married a hometown legend.

After settling down, his mom called him downstairs to drink some coffee and she wanted to show him something that his dad had left him. She was so happy to see James, because he resembled his dad in many ways, and she said that it was too bad we did not call you junior. They both laughed. After talking for a while, she said, follow me to the garage that was built in the backyard by his dad and other members of the church. She told James that when it was completed, there was a great celebration. People stayed late that day and just had a wonderful time. She said you would have thought that they were building Noah's ark. She opened the door and there under a dusty beat-up looking tarp was a beauty just like it was new - his old 1968 red Mustang convertible. He was such in shock that he could not speak and just started to cry. His mom came by his side, and she told him, that his dad had it completely restored. She said that it was a mess, because of the wreck, but his dad hoped that one day he would ride again. She said that his dad had enjoyed many rides down that countryside.

He climbed in and started the engine, and it was the sound of the past. It was the first car that he ever owned and had paid for while working at the hardware store. Gracie heard the engine of the car and came out to see what it was. James told her to hop in and ride down memory lane with him. The top was down, and Gracie was admiring the different colors of the trees and of course the radio station was on K-Love. After the ride, they were so tired from the journey that they had just taken and went to bed that evening and did not wake up until one o'clock that next day. James' mom let them sleep and had prepared a wonderful lunch. His mom approached him and asked him if he had prayed about taking over the church and he said yes that he had and was going to talk to the church elders. So, he called the church secretary and asked for an appointment to be set up and discuss the plans for the church. Gracie was going to start looking for a job and try to find out what certificates she needed to complete to be able to practice as a physician assistant in the state of Montana. She went to the nearest veteran clinic to inquire on how she could transfer her practice from San Antonio, Texas to Montana. They directed her to human resources and started the paperwork so that she could get hired at the clinic. They desperately needed medical staff as the population of veterans needing care was growing in their area. Gracie was hired and started to work as soon as she could so that she could have medical benefits. James did not need any medical insurance; he just transferred his medical records from San Antonio to Missoula's veteran clinic. Gracie and James prayed that day and they saw Gods plan being developed in their lives. He had accepted the position of the pastor of the church and Gracie was hired at the veteran clinic. A couple of years had gone by, and Gracie came up to James and asked if they could start a family and James asked if they could start right then! She just laughed and said no silly, I have to go to work but tonight fix me a good Mexican dinner. That evening James wanted to play a joke on Gracie and had bought Taco Bell and placed some fancy silverware and fancy plates for that evening. When Gracie came home and saw what was on the table, she was mad, and James told her that it was just a joke. He had fixed some meat fajitas marinated in his secret ingredients, rice and beans, tortillas, Pico de Gallo, cheese dip with chips, the whole fixings. After a few months had gone by, she was expecting, and the couple was so happy. As her pregnancy progressed, she started developing complications, and when she went to her doctor for a follow up, the doctor told her that her blood pressure had gone up and gave Gracie orders to stay off her feet and recommended her to stay in bed as much as possible. On her delivery day, Gracie was in her room along with James. The time came and the doctor told her to push but noticed that Gracie's blood pressure was going up and she was struggling to breathe. The doctor told James to leave the room and told the nurses to call other doctors for help. James was in the waiting room along with his mother and other members of the church, praying for God's hand to be upon Gracie and the baby. James had told his mom that the baby's name would be Mary Jo Dawn Robinson, because they had found out earlier that it would be a baby girl.

After hours of waiting, the baby was wheeled off to the neonatal intensive care for observation and care. Finally, the doctor came out and told James and his family that Gracie did not make it, she had suffered such a heart attack that the team could not save her. James broke down immediately and his mom knew all she could do was hold him. The church members gathered around him and all wept. Mary Jo was finally discharged from the hospital and James did not want anything to do with her. He blamed the baby for the loss of his wife. He even questioned God through all of this and was starting to decline in his spiritual life. His sermons were not passionate anymore and his congregation started to notice and complained to the elders of the church. Some church members left the church and were looking to attend other churches. James started to drink and take pain pills to try to drown out his pain. He was let go at his church and His mom was raising Mary Jo, because James did not want anything to do with the baby.

Years had passed and Mary Jo was beautiful and was now in high school, without the leadership of a mom or dad. Her grandma did the best she could to raise her.

Mary Jo started hanging around the wrong crowd and was getting into early sex, alcohol and drugs. There was a man, driving around the high school who noticed her and he slowly became her friend. She was looking for a dad figure, but this man was just looking for a young lady to bring her into the evil sex trafficking world. He promised her an education and that she would never be without a home or food, so she went with him only to find out that she was being sold to another bad man. She could not escape or have any communication with anybody, because she was transported to different states for sexual use as a prostitute. The bad man told her that if she tried to escape that he would hunt her down and kill her and all members of the family. Mary Jo had become friends with another victim called Jewel and they held on to each other when they were locked up in their room with other females.

One night Jewell did not come back, and Mary Jo found out that she had been overdosed and she did not make it. The bad man had told all the girls that she tried to escape and so they killed her in order to put fear into the women that were in the room. That night

Mary Jo got on her knees and looked up and started to pray. The other girls noticed her, and they gathered around as a group and asked God for help in their circumstances and to deliver them from this slavery. That night all the girls came to Christ and decided that night to have a small secret session and learn about the Bible. One of the girls had found a Gideon Bible in one of the rooms and snuck it in for them to read and learn more of the story of Jesus Christ. One day Mary Jo's prayer came to fruition, and she had the opportunity to escape. A pastor at a local church noticed her and asked if she was in danger. She had to be careful, because many eyes were upon her, but she slipped him a note and said, yes. The pastor told her to hang on and he would devise a plan to help her escape. So, he pretended to solicit her and paid the bad man some cash. The pastor had other women help him from his congregation and Mary Jo was able to escape. This church's sole mission was to help young men and women get out of the sex trafficking business.

Now, the bad man was getting suspicious and went barging into the room only to find it empty. They had escaped through the back window. He started cursing and wanted to kill the pastor who had helped Mary Jo escape. He alerted his gang to be on the lookout for Mary Jo and the pastor. He wanted both of them dead. So, he set a bounty on Mary Jo for ten thousand dollars for anybody that would bring her back alive.

Mary Jo's life changed that day, because the church took her in and kept her safe. She came to know Jesus Christ that day and had seen God answer her prayers. The congregation had called the police for help and hoped maybe Mary Jo could provide any information that would lead to rescuing the other girls. By the time the police got to the location she had given them, it was empty.

Mary Jo was pregnant and had not told the bad man about it, because he would do something drastic to Mary Jo, so the church helped pay to have the baby at a local hospital and provided her and the baby with nourishment for quite some time. She had a church family that loved her and kept her safe. One day the bad man found the pastor and beat him up for information and the church members found out and gave Mary Jo a car so that she could get out of town and start a new life with her baby.

It is so sad to know that human sex trafficking will never come to an end due to the sinful nature of man. Until Jesus comes again, all the sin of this world will not stop. According to Psalm 1:5-6 (NIV) Therefore the wicked will not stand in the judgment nor sinners in the assembly of the righteous. For the Lord watches over the way of the righteous but the way of the wicked will perish. According to Etactics report:

- 79% of human trafficking is sex trafficking.
- 77% of sex trafficking victims are female.
  - Another 17% are male.
  - The rest are under the label of "unknown."
- There are approximately 35 million victims of sex trafficking on any given day.
- Sex trafficking can yield a return on investment between 100% to 1,000%.
- The sex trafficking industry alone has a market value of $99 billion.
  - This means that the sex trafficking industry is larger than the global cocaine market.

We as Christians around the world need to be on our

knees and pray for victims in this industry. We need to pray for healing for those victims that have gone through it. There is a lot of emotional damage incurred from this trauma in their lives and I believe that Jesus can wrap His loving arms around them and be a part of their healing process. If you know of anybody that is need of help or are a victim of this market, please call the National Human Trafficking Hotline at: 1-888-373-7888.

Chapter 10
Going Home

Revelation 21:4 (NIV)
"He will wipe away every tear from their eyes, and death shall be no more, neither shall there be mourning, nor crying, nor pain anymore, for the former things have passed away."

It was a beautiful day traveling down the back roads of Tennessee. Mary Jo and her three-year old daughter Grace were in an old Impala that had barely made it through several states. Mary Jo was running away from her past. She did not want to look back, but the bad man was still looking for and was furious at her and wanted to kill her and her daughter. According to him, she had broken the code and deserved to die. He had even put a bounty on her head. Her number-one concern was now to raise her daughter away from drugs, alcohol, smoking, and prostitution. Mary Jo was forced into that life, and it was all she knew.

She continued to do this profession to have money to provide food and clothing for her beautiful daughter. Mary Jo used to be so beautiful, but the toll of men abusing her and using drugs had made her age rapidly.

Her daughter Grace had beautiful blue eyes, blonde hair that the reflection of the sun caused to look like gold strands. Her little smile could brighten up a dark room and her voice could make the birds start to chirp. God had spent an extra time in molding this little one.

Mary Jo could have sworn that at times when she saw her child in the driver's mirror, she could see wings on Grace. She was Mary Jo's little angel. They had traveled many miles, and they were both hungry and the car needed gas. Mary Jo saw a sign for the next town called Springfield and decided that she would stop there to rest and find a man to supplement her material needs. While driving she started to put on makeup and straighten her hair and put on some cheap perfume, she had shop lifted at a local dollar store. She had mastered the art of stealing anything she wanted to make her survive. She drove to the outskirts of town and saw a diner. She walked in with her little girl and sat down and put in a small order for coffee and small juice for Grace. While waiting for the server to return with the drinks she started scoping like an eagle on its prey.

She saw a young server's helper busting tables and started to wink at him to get his attention. She started caressing her own body to lure him to her and it worked. She asked him his name. He said, "I am Steve and I live in this town and my father owns the diner."

She was in luck. She gave him her sob story and told him that she would show him a good time, if he could pay for their food and gas money. He obliged. She told him to meet her around the back and she would be waiting in her car. She placed the car seat in the front with Grace, while she conducted business. Steve was innocent and this was his first time with a woman. Of course, Steve fell in love and gave her enough money for several gallons of gas and food. He even invited her to come to his apartment, so that she could shower and get some rest with Grace. Mary Jo and Grace fell fast asleep. It was the first time that Mary Jo had felt peace in a long time. The next morning Steve had woken up and wanted to cook breakfast for the girls. The smell of bacon and eggs awakened Mary Jo. She and Grace approached the table and ate all that was in front of them.

Steve had told Mary Jo to stay a few days and rest and that he would take care of them. Grace just loved Steve's gentleness and loved playing with him. Mary Jo dreamed of the day that she could find a good man to settle down with and who would be a good father to Grace. Steve had to go back to work but told the girls to make themselves at home. He told Mary Jo that he would take her and show her around town when he got off. When he finally got home, he took both girls out around town and to the county fair. They had a wonderful time and while returning to the car a young girl approached her, gave her a Bible, and told her that Jesus loved her and walked away. Steve told Mary Jo that this was a Jesus-loving town and she smirked at him and told him that she did not want to hear about Jesus. She asked Steve where was Jesus? She told him about her father the preacher who had refused to love her and he would preach about the Lord but did not follow Him according to Scripture. There was silence on the way back to the apartment.

The next morning Steve awoke, just to realize that the girls had already gone. Mary Jo was not going to rest until she reached Mexico. She wanted to leave the country. She had tears rolling down her cheeks, because she thought that she had fallen asleep and dreamt that she had found the place to settle down but could not. Grace asked her, "What is wrong, Mommy?"

Mary Jo, responded, "Those are tears of hope, honey."

While traveling the back roads, they saw many animals, beautiful foliage and friendly people waving at them. She was on her way to Memphis.

Paul was finishing a meeting in Murfreesboro. This meeting was about how to initiate a business and maintain it. He had retired from the Navy and wanted to utilize his talents. It was a long weekend, and he was ready to go home. He got into his car and typed into his Garmin to route the most scenic route to Memphis.

He wanted to utilize the beauty that Tennessee provided. He stopped at a local gas station to refuel and get a big bag of his favorite chips. He did all of this, because he did not know if the route had any gas stations or chips.

After gathering his supplies, Paul prayed for blessings and a safe trip back home. He prayed to God that He would use him in any way that He saw fit to do. He also prayed for all the drivers on the road and that they would seek Jesus daily. So, off Paul went on his new adventure and wanting to be in his own bed by nightfall. He had driven for about two hours and was admiring what God had created just for his eyes. He marveled at the picturesque scenes that God had painted. The sun was going down, and it was getting slightly dark and the lights on his car had come on. Paul was driving peacefully on this stretch of road with no traffic coming or going, when at a distance he saw a figure beside the road and he thought that it could be some animal wanting to cross the road, so he slowed down. He did not want to have an accident on this road, with no one in sight to help if he did.

As he got closer, he slowed down even more, just to see that the figure was not an animal, but the shadow of a little girl.

Paul immediately stopped his car and put his flashers on. He paused for a moment and prayed for guidance in this situation.

He had been trained as a medic while in the service, so he knew first aid. He was concerned that it could be a setup, that if he got out of his car he would be robbed, and that the little girl was a decoy. God had reminded him of the prayer that he had prayed at the gas station. He got out of his car and noticed that the little girl was covered in blood. Paul immediately kicked into his medic mode and started to ask the little girl for her name and if she was injured. The little girl was shivering, and Paul had a blanket in the car he wrapped around her. She said that her name was Grace and that her mommy was down there. Paul dialed 911 and could barely get a signal, but finally reached an operator. Paul told the operator that he had no idea where he was, but that he needed an ambulance right now.

He told the operator that he would put his cell phone on top of his car and hoped that they could ping his location. He comforted the little girl and told her that he would find her mom and to please stay in the car for safety. Grace obliged and fell asleep in the back seat. It had gotten dark, and Paul did not have any lighting to guide him to the wreck.

Paul started praying to God to provide lighting and at that very moment the stars came out and they were bright as though it was daylight. That night, Paul followed a star that led him down an embankment, a drainage gap and through a barb wire fence that the vehicle had torn and saw that it had crashed into a big tree. He could see the taillights of the vehicle and when he had reached the passenger side, he had to use all his might to open the door. When he got in to check on the lady that was driving, the inside of the car was covered in blood. The driver had lost a lot of blood due to her severe injuries. She was barely alive and was gasping for air. Paul told her who he was and that her daughter was safe.

She barely could speak, and he knew that she was dying. He told her that he could not get her out of the car, because her legs were pinned. Paul told her that he could not save her, but that there was a God who could. He told her about Jesus and that He could save her, and she could spend the rest of eternity with Him. He prayed the prayer of salvation, and she followed the words with her lips.

There was peace and she was going home. Before she took her last breath, she had pointed towards the glove compartment and as he opened it, there was a stack of undelivered letters addressed to a man in Montana. Paul told her that he would take care of them and make sure that they got mailed. The glory of God filled that vehicle that night and Paul knew that God had brought him out there for a purpose of saving a life for Jesus.

Paul started going back slowly up to the road and back to the safety of his car. The little girl was sound asleep. He waited for hours and still there was no sign of any emergency vehicle. He got on the phone with the operator and explained to her what had happened.

Paul told the operator that the lady had gone home to be with the Lord and there were tears coming from the operator and the department. Finally, he told the operator that he could see blue lights flashing and coming towards him. Paul flashed his lights many times and finally the state trooper got out and told him that help was coming.

Finally, the fire truck and ambulance arrived, and Paul had told the emergency personnel that the driver did not make it. Paul grabbed the little girl and gave her over to the emergency personnel. Paul provided all the necessary information to the state trooper and gave him the letters and his phone number just in case that person wanted to know about this pastor's daughter. On his way home, Paul just prayed and sobbed tears of joy because a soul was going home to be with the Lord. He had reached Memphis and was exhausted from the trip and could hardly wait to get to bed. As a retired medical person, he had gone out with a bang and was glad that God had used him as a vessel to reach out to this lady that he had encountered. Before going to bed, he sat down to read his Bible and it brought him to Romans 10 and what stuck out to him was verse nine.

"That if you confess with your mouth, Jesus is Lord and believe in your heart that God raised him from the dead, you will be saved." Paul was so tired that he could not finish his study and fell asleep with his Bible clutched in his right hand.

Several months had passed by when he got a phone call from an unknown number. Paul was hesitant to answer but did anyway and a still voice asked if he was Paul. Of course, said Paul, and the man proceeded to tell him that he was the father of the lady that had passed away in the accident and was the grandfather of Grace that Paul had rescued. He also told me that he had read all the letters that were written to him and started to cry. He could not hold himself and apologized on the phone and Paul said take your time, I am still here and listening. As the pastor composed himself, he proceeded to tell the story of how he had so much bitterness towards Mary Jo and blamed her for the death of his wife. His only regret was that he was not a good father and now he could not say he was sorry to his daughter.

He wanted me to tell him if Mary Jo had said anything and I told him that she could not due to her injuries.

He thanked me and told me that Grace was with him, and that God had given him another opportunity to raise a granddaughter.

He had paid for Mary Jo's body to be flown to his hometown and buried her next to her mom. It was a lonely funeral, but you could sense the Holy Spirit's presence. After talking for a while, he made a statement that Mary Jo had gone home and hung up. Paul paused for a moment and thanked the Lord for using him as a vessel to find grace and that heaven that had received another soul home.

The End

References

70+ Unimaginable Human Trafficking Statistics **in The US**

https://etactics.com/blog/human-trafficking-statistics-in-the-us

Sep 16, 2021.

About the Author

Raul and Tammy are happily married and spend time with grandchildren and family. Our prayer is that no matter what you are going through you constantly seek Him. Focus on God's goodness, His infinite, unchanging, and perfect love for you. Tammy and I give God all the glory and praise in good times and bad times. Will you run to God? He is ready to overwhelm you with His grace, acceptance and forgiveness. Will you seek His grace? He is waiting.

www.ingramcontent.com/pod-product-compliance
Lightning Source LLC
Chambersburg PA
CBHW051242160726
47994CB00002B/992